TWISTAPLOT

2

THE TRAIN OF TERROR

Louise Munro Foley

ILLUSTRATIONS BY DAVID FEBLAND

SCHOLASTIC BOOK SERVICES

New York Toronto London Auckland Sydney Tokyo

ISBN 0-590-32499-3

Copyright © 1982 by Louise Munro Foley. All rights reserved. Published by Scholastic Book Services, a division of Scholastic Inc.

12 11 10 9 8 7 6 5 4 3 2 1   11   2 3 4 5 6/8

Printed in the U. S. A.   01

This book is affectionately dedicated to Don Foley, who made a choice a few years back and has been riding a train of terror ever since.

BEWARE!!!
DO NOT READ THIS
BOOK FROM
BEGINNING TO END

You will have countless adventures on *The Train of Terror*, but *only* if you follow the directions at the bottom of each page. Think carefully before you flip a page. A wrong turn could mean danger or even death! The right one could make you famous.

What happens depends on you. If you get into trouble, turn back and choose a different way out. If you're having a good time, keep going!

So climb aboard — follow the directions on each page — and brace yourself for hazardous escapades and some weird people!

Turn to PAGE 2.

You are boarding a train in your hometown to spend the summer with your Aunt Kate in Twin Falls, Idaho. Your mother has packed you a lunch and insists on staying with you until the train leaves. She even tries to kiss you good-bye in the station with all the other people watching.

You get around that by pretending you are whispering a secret in her ear while she is kissing you. At the same time, you are watching a tall, thin bald man in a black suit, who is watching a beautiful blonde lady in a red dress. She has a large pet carrier sitting on the platform beside her.

The bald man has a long diagonal scar running across his forehead from one side to the other.

You wonder whether the lady has a dog or a cat in the carrier.

Please turn to PAGE 4.

The train whistles as it rolls into the station. Because your mother is giving you last-minute instructions, you are the last person to climb on.

The car is crowded but strangely quiet. No one is talking. As you move down the aisle, you look at the passengers, but everyone stares straight ahead like robots.

There are only three seats left. One beside Beautiful Lady, one beside Scarface, and one beside an elderly lady wearing a veiled purple hat, which hides her face. Elderly Lady has her knitting on the seat beside her and looks like an old grouch. You don't want to get stuck there. It's going to be a long ride.

If you decide to sit by Beautiful Lady, turn to PAGE 6.

If you decide to sit by Scarface, turn to PAGE 9.

Keeping as still as you can so you won't give away your position, you look around. You need to divert Beautiful Lady's attention so you can get out.

Propped up between a large box and a suitcase, you see a pair of skis, standing on end. Hoping the owner will forgive you, you slither across the top of the trunks and kick the skis with your left foot. They teeter, then crash right on top of the pet carrier!

Two shots ring out. One grazes your arm — the other zings into the pet carrier.

You feel terrible. That poor animal has suffered enough from being cooped up. Now you're responsible for its getting shot!

Unmindful of your own safety, you scramble over and open the door to the pet carrier. Inside is a small, very damaged computer.

A noise. You glance up just in time.

Beautiful Lady is aiming at you again!

You duck behind a metal drum just as the door to the baggage car opens, and Scarface enters. Behind him is the conductor.

"Drop it!" says Scarface.

Beautiful Lady's gun drops to the floor with a clunk.

Who are these weirdos? Turn to PAGE 104.

You stop by Beautiful Lady. The pet carrier is on the floor by her feet.

"Is this seat taken?" you ask politely.

Your voice sounds very loud in the quiet coach and you look around, embarrassed. Elderly Lady, who is in the seat ahead, has turned around and is watching you closely. Scarface is seated across the aisle. He is observing you out of the corner of his eye. You feel uncomfortable.

"Is this seat taken?" you repeat in a whisper.

Beautiful Lady glances up at you quickly, with a mean expression on her face.

"No," she says, curtly. "But . . ."

Go on to PAGE 7.

You sit down without waiting for her to finish, and as you do, you drop your lunch bag. It hits the pet carrier and falls on the floor by the door.

You reach down to pick it up, and Beautiful Lady grabs your arm.

"Leave it there!" she orders.

If you decide to pick up your lunch, turn to PAGE 10.

If you choose to leave it on the floor, turn to PAGE 11.

You'll have to go back for the girl later. You would be no help to her in your drugged condition.

Mustering your last ounce of will, you take one last look back at Beautiful Lady. She's desperately punching out numbers on that strange keyboard. What is that thing, anyway? Some kind of mind-control device? Whatever it is, it doesn't work between the two cars.

Exhausted, you sink into the nearest empty seat. You shut your eyes. A baby is crying at the front of the coach, and someone near you sneezes. Thank heavens! The people in this car are normal.

You open your eyes. These passengers are not only normal, they're look-alikes of the people you saw in the other car! Only now they seem like real people.

Right next to you is Scarface, in the black suit. Wasn't he on the last car? He offers you a stick of gum. You stare at him.

"Is something wrong?" he asks.

"You ... I saw you on the coach at the end of the train," you stammer.

"You are mistaken," he replies kindly. "This is the last coach on the train."

"That's impossible. I saw you, I know I did," you cry desperately.

"Nothing is impossible on The Train of Terror," he replies.

THE END

You smile as you drop into the seat beside Scarface, but his head only jerks to one side in an abrupt acknowledgment.

"Hi," you say.

His mouth opens slightly, but no sound comes out. You wonder if he has laryngitis. Your kid brother had it last April. You had seven wonderful days of peace.

You take a crossword puzzle book out of your pocket and a package of sunflower seeds from your lunch bag and try to concentrate on solving a cryptogram — but you feel very uncomfortable.

You look up, aware that someone is staring at you. Without smiling, Scarface reaches over to snatch the pencil from your hand.

If you let him take the pencil, turn to PAGE 30.

If you hold on to it, turn to PAGE 105.

You have absolutely no intention of leaving your lunch on the floor. It's been a long time since breakfast. Besides, there's a package of sunflower seeds and an apple in there that you want to nibble on right now. What gives Beautiful Lady the right to order you around, anyway?

You shake loose from her grip and lean over to pick up your lunch bag. It rips as you grasp it, and your apple rolls under the seat in front. The bag of sunflower seeds catches on the door handle of the pet carrier.

If you pick up the sunflower seeds first, turn to PAGE 59.

If you decide to retrieve your apple first, turn to PAGE 60.

You look at Beautiful Lady, puzzled by the urgency in her voice.

"It's my lunch," you say, explaining about the bag you dropped.

She leans over and speaks close to your ear.

"I'm sorry for being so abrupt," she says, "but you must not touch it. It could be contaminated."

Indignantly, you pull away from her grasp. "My mother does not pack contaminated lunches," you declare.

Beautiful Lady smiles. "Of course not." She lowers her voice. "It was not contaminated until you dropped it. My . . . pet . . . is really a dangerous chemical."

Astonished, you look from her beautiful face down to the box on the floor.

"What's in there?" you whisper.

She digs a gloved hand into her tapestry handbag and extracts a slim brown leather wallet, which she flips open.

"Military secret," she responds in a hushed tone.

The card in her wallet identifies her as L. Smythe, secret service agent.

"But you touched it!" you protest, not wishing to be taken for a fool.

Please continue reading on PAGE 12.

"But I am wearing protective clothing," she says. "Look." She peels off a glove and shows you a special lining. "My clothing has a lead shield."

You instinctively move closer to the aisle, away from the pet carrier.

She smiles. "You are safe where you are," she says. "As long as I sit between you and . . . it."

You're not sure you believe what she says.

You are hungry, and your expression must show how miserable you feel, for L. Smythe pats your knee sympathetically.

"I owe you a lunch," she says, reading your mind. "Come with me to the dining car, and I'll treat you to a meal."

If you decide to accept her offer, turn to PAGE 75.

If you decide to go hungry, turn to PAGE 76.

You snatch your apple from between Elderly Lady's shoes. As you quickly back out from under the seat, you hear a faint, muffled cry coming from the pet carrier.

"Help!"

If you decide to investigate, turn to PAGE 47.

If you decide that enough weird things have happened already, and you want to leave well enough alone, turn to PAGE 26.

14

You squint into the dark interior of the pet carrier, but you can see nothing. As you pretend to fumble for your sunflower seeds, you lean in closer. You feel a sharp pain across the bridge of your nose and rear back quickly. As you do, a long blue-and-silver snake glides out of the carrier and slithers noiselessly down the aisle.

"Help!" you cry, holding your head. "Get the conductor! I've been bitten by a snake. There's a snake loose in this coach!"

Beautiful Lady grabs the back of your neck and pulls you into the seat.

"Be quiet," she commands. Her grip on you is like steel. Frightened, you look around. No one appears to have heard your cries except Elderly Lady and Scarface. But they do not move. They only watch.

Beautiful Lady fumbles in her handbag and brings out a bottle of pills.

"Antivenin," she whispers at you. "Take one!"

She forces a small blue-and-silver capsule into your mouth.

If you decide to swallow the pill, turn to PAGE 66.

If you decide to spit it out and run for the conductor, turn to PAGE 68.

Scarface gives you a fleeting look of urgency, and his eyes plead with you to do as he asks. With a sigh, you get up and walk through the coach to the baggage car ahead. Might as well explore. You weren't anxious to stay where you were, anyway.

The train is crowded, but there is no car as full as the one that you just left. And no car is as eerily quiet, either.

You pass a family playing a word game, a group of sailors engaged in a hand of poker, and a cowboy strumming a guitar. They are all friendly — nothing like the people in your coach.

You reach the baggage car and cautiously look around to see if a porter or the conductor has seen you.

A red-and-white metal sign on the door reads:

AUTHORIZED PERSONNEL ONLY

You push the heavy door open and enter.

All authorized readers may turn to PAGE 53.

What a strange man! you think.

Scarface is leaning back in the seat, his eyes are closed, and his hands are on his knees. He appears to be concentrating very hard, but he is not moving a muscle.

Maybe he is sick.

"Excuse me, sir," you say. "Are you ill?"

His eyes flutter open, and you know he has heard you, but he does not even move his head.

"Shall I get the conductor?" you ask. "You don't look well."

"Perhaps I can help," says Beautiful Lady, who has been eavesdropping. "I am a doctor."

"You are?" you say, surprised at this information. All the doctors you know are male and bald.

She smiles and nods. "Trade seats with me," she says. "I will examine him."

It sounds good to you. There's obviously something wrong with Scarface. You are about to move when you feel a viselike grip on your arm. You look at Scarface. Fear is mirrored in his glassy eyes. He is trying to prevent you from moving.

If you let Beautiful Lady trade seats with you, turn to PAGE 55.

If you decide to stay beside Scarface, turn to PAGE 56.

18

You wait nervously in the seat beside the snoring Cowboy for what seems like hours. You watch the door closely and wonder why Beautiful Lady didn't follow you. And again you wonder — *what is in the pet carrier?*

Finally, the conductor comes into the car. You motion him over and whisper what has happened so you won't waken Cowboy.

The conductor shakes his head and frowns.

"You kids are all alike," he growls. "Makin' up stories to get people all riled up."

"But it's true!" you insist.

"Prove it," he says.

If you decide to give up in disgust and pretend the whole thing was a bad dream, turn to PAGE 77.

If you decide to prove your story to the conductor, turn to PAGE 80.

Something in Cowboy's tone tells you to go with him.

"Never mind," you say to the conductor.

You and Cowboy sit down at a small table in the club car and order root beer.

"Yer so smart that yer jeopardizin' my roundup," says Cowboy with a grin.

"What do you mean?" you ask.

"I'm Clint Westrock, U.S. Marshal. I'm after that quartet. I can't take all four of them in alone, so I'm jist bidin' my time till we get to Idaho."

"Quartet?" you say, puzzled.

"Yep. The lady in the red dress, the man with the scar, and the old lady in the purple hat, who's really Studs Monigan ridin' incognito, and the conductor."

"No wonder he didn't want to check out my story!" you exclaim.

"They robbed a bank back east," says Cowboy. "Money's in the pet carrier. I could take 'em in right now, with help. I could deputize you, but it could be dangerous. What do you say?"

He gives you time to think it over.

___

If you decide to help Cowboy, turn to PAGE 86.

If you decide it would be too dangerous, turn to PAGE 87.

You go limp, dropping into the seat by Elderly Lady, and tuck your legs up under you, Indian fashion.

You feel it's your duty to warn your seat companion about the snake. She is looking out the window at the scenery. Gently, you touch her arm, and she turns to hear what you have to say.

Only then do you see that the snake is already coiled around her neck. She strokes it lovingly and smiles as it strikes out at the hollow in your neck.

You slump in the seat, knowing that this is the end for you. Your mother always said your curiosity would get you into trouble.

Big trouble.

Your mother was right.

Curiosity kills more than cats.

THE END

You hold your breath and stare at Elderly Lady. Her face is strange when she speaks. Her jaws look as though they are wired together, and her words come out without any feeling. You study her hand, beckoning you over. The skin is smooth and firm and plastic-looking, like a mannequin's.

You force yourself down the aisle to the door and wrench it open.

"There's a snake loose in there," you gasp, gulping in the fresh air. "And a woman back there who tried to drug me! I think she turned everyone into robots or something. Stop her!" you plead to the conductor.

He stares at you with glassy eyes, and his mouth moves mechanically up and down.

"That is impossible," he says.

As he approaches, you back away. You grasp the metal frame and vault over the half-door. Tucking your knees up as you drop to the ground, you roll away from the tracks. All those boring sit-ups in gym have paid off!

You lie there for a few moments, watching as the Train of Terror glides out of sight. Then you stand up and brush yourself off.

This is your lucky day. Idaho is only 800 miles up the track.

You hope Aunt Kate won't wait dinner for you.

THE END ✓

"Please sit down," you say to Scarface, sticking out your tongue at L. Smythe.

Since you cleverly entwined your feet in the rungs of the chair opposite you while L. Smythe was delivering her threatening speech, you are able to act as you speak.

With one sharp upward kick, you tip the chair holding the pet carrier backward, just as L. Smythe triggers the poison dart. Noiselessly, it imbeds itself in the ceiling of the dining car.

At the same time, Scarface springs into action. Grabbing the edge of the white linen tablecloth, he flings it up and over L. Smythe's head. As she struggles to free herself from the cloth, security guards arrive and take her and her pet carrier into custody.

"Quick thinking," says Scarface.

"It was nothing," you reply, offering him some pizza.

He sits down opposite you and takes out a deck of cards. The two of you play Go Fish until you reach Twin Falls.

You win.

Please continue reading on PAGE 67.

"I'm sorry, but we're expecting my father to join us," you say to Scarface, stalling for time.

Under the table, where no one can see what you're doing, you are placing your feet on the rungs of the chair that holds the pet carrier. You're pretty adept at it. At home, you do it to your younger sister during dinner, and she gets furious.

You smile at Scarface. "He's a colonel in the army," you continue. "Stationed at Fort Benjamin Harrison, Indiana."

You're getting pretty good at lies, too.

As you speak, you kick the chair up, tipping the pet carrier. The poison dart flies harmlessly to the ceiling of the coach and imbeds itself in a hardwood molding.

Beautiful Lady tries to run, but Scarface stops her flight.

"Quick thinking," he says to you as he handcuffs her. "I was wondering how I could disarm her dart thrower. You'll get a citation for this!"

Please turn to PAGE 100.

24

"Stop her!" Elderly Lady yells in a deep voice.

She is trying to climb over the seat, but her sling pump is caught in the seat cushion. "Don't let her take that pill!" Elderly Lady's purple hat falls off, and you notice that she has a mustache.

Turn to PAGE 48, please.

It's your fault that Beautiful Lady's pet escaped.

You look up from the floor to apologize for freeing her bird by mistake, but you are silenced by her look of rage. She reaches for something in her tapestry handbag — a gun, perhaps? You sense that she means business, so you duck back into the cramped space under the seat. There is no place to hide.

This is it, you think. Curtains.

You peek out.

She is not holding a gun but a bottle of pills.

Frantically, she tugs at the cap. It is the childproof kind that only a child can open. She manages to yank it off.

Look over to PAGE 24.

You keep munching on your apple. The cry from the pet carrier comes again.

"Help! Help, help!"

"Listen," you say to Beautiful Lady.

"I don't hear anything," she replies.

You decide it must be the unfamiliar sound of the train. You pick up the newspaper lying on the seat and thumb through the pages, looking for your horoscope.

On page three, you notice a picture of someone who looks vaguely familiar.

It is Beautiful Lady!

The headline reads: *Beautiful Jewel Thief at Large.*

Loretta Swensen and her ventriloquist accomplice are being sought following the robbery of a Boston gem merchant. The merchant was wounded during the robbery and the thieves escaped, carrying the gems in a pet carrier.

No wonder she didn't want you near it! It's full of jewels! And *ventriloquist accomplice* — that explains the talking cage!

You close the paper quickly. Beautiful Lady is looking at you. Does she know that you know? Who is her accomplice?

If you decide that it's Elderly Lady, turn to PAGE 65.

If you decide that it's Scarface, turn to PAGE 54.

You get up, anyway, despite Beautiful Lady's warning, but Scarface moves to block your path. You push him out of the way and run down the aisle. The coach is empty now, except for you, the jewel thieves, and the strange Elderly Lady with hairy legs.

You are wondering why Scarface does not follow you. You hear scuffling and turn around. Scarface and Beautiful Lady are wrestling with Elderly Lady!

Your conscience tweaks at you.

What is the honorable and wise thing to do?

If you decide to be honorable and wise, turn to PAGE 45.

If you decide to take a rain check on the wrestling match, turn to PAGE 96.

Will you be in time to save the little girl? What can you use as a weapon against the snake? Your hand grasps the heavy buckle on your belt.

Fumbling, you slip your belt through the loops and curl your hand around it, leaving the buckle end swinging.

Dragging one heavy foot after the other, you reach the seat where the child is sleeping. It's so hard to move and to concentrate on your dangerous mission. You're sure now that Beautiful Lady must have drugged you with her so-called antivenin pill. You'll have to figure out why later. Right now you have to get that snake!

You rattle the belt buckle to attract the snake, then stand poised and ready. Its beady eyes focus on you as it slithers off the child and prepares to strike.

Zap!

With perfect timing, you lash out with the belt at precisely the same moment that the snake darts at you. The force of the buckle throws it to the floor, where it jerks convulsively three times, then dies.

Go on to PAGE 29.

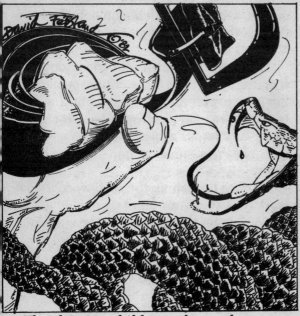

The sleeping child stretches and yawns.

"Hi," she says, smiling at you.

Suddenly, you feel much better as energy surges through your body. A change has come over the whole coach. People are moving now, rustling newspapers, shuffling cards, conversing. Elderly Lady picks up her knitting, and the needles click together musically as she guides the wool. Scarface is smiling.

You look at Beautiful Lady. She sits rigid in her seat, like a mannequin — a robot. Puzzled, you look down at the snake.

Please turn to PAGE 35.

Mystified by Scarface's action, but curious, too, you watch as he clumsily indicates that he wants your crossword puzzle book as well!

You hand it to him and glance over at Beautiful Lady. She is watching you closely, her piercing blue eyes missing nothing. She is resting one hand on top of her pet carrier, and you wonder again if it contains a dog or a cat. You smile at her, but she turns away.

Scarface is pushing the crossword puzzle book back into your hand. Scrawled across the cover, he has painstakingly written:

DANGER

IN BOX

GO

BAGGAGE CAR

RUN

Is this some sort of joke? You study his scarred face to see if he's kidding.

___

If you decide to go to the baggage car, turn to PAGE 16.

If you decide that he's kidding, turn to PAGE 17.

You jump up and run. Footsteps pound down the aisle behind you. The train starts to move again just as you reach the door. You jump to the platform below and run inside the station, looking back over your shoulder.

The man dressed as the old woman is hanging from the doorway, waving the stiletto at you. You're glad it wasn't a gun, or you'd have been a goner by now. You're also glad he was wearing pumps or he would have caught you easily.

You lean on the counter as you breathlessly tell the stationmaster your story.

That night, you watch the eleven o'clock news and see the dramatic capture of Beautiful Lady and Elderly Lady. You are on TV, too, in a segment filmed while you were giving a statement at the local police station that afternoon.

The next day, you get on a train for Idaho.

Nobody kisses you good-bye at the station.

It should be an uneventful ride.

THE END

"Yes!" you shout at Cowboy. "You do believe me! You saw her, too!"

"Didn't say that," he drawls. "But I'd be willin' to check it out. You want to go take a look?"

You eye him suspiciously. He could be making fun of you again, or he might really want to help. But do you want to risk going back into that coach again?

If you decide to accept Cowboy's offer, turn to PAGE 94.

If you decide to decline, turn to PAGE 58.

"You read page three very carefully," says Beautiful Lady ominously.

"I don't remember," you say.

"Do you remember seeing a picture of me?" she demands.

"I don't think so," you reply, getting up.

"Where are you going?" she asks as you inch out into the aisle, toward Scarface.

"I'm going to sit over here so I can ... see the scenery on the other side of the train," you mumble.

You sit down beside Scarface, who has been watching with quiet amusement.

"Fine," snaps Beautiful Lady. "But you will get off when I do. You know too much." Her tone is threatening.

You know you're going to have to do something fast. You turn to Scarface.

"She's a thief!" you cry in a loud voice. "She robbed a gem merchant in Boston!"

"Is that right?" says Scarface with a patronizing smile. "How do you know?"

You are about to tell him that you read it in the paper when you realize that his lips have not moved — only his Adam's apple — and his words are coming from the pet carrier. He is the ventriloquist!

Scarface is her accomplice!

Turn to PAGE 40.

The conductor shakes his head and looks disapprovingly at you.

"You're all mixed up," he says. "Only person in that car with a pet carrier is a bald, scarfaced man in a black suit."

"No!" you say, bewildered. "Come on! I'll show you!"

Cowboy, awakened by the argument, puts his hand on your shoulder.

"Simmer down, pardner," he says. "Let's you 'n' me go up to the club car and get some root beer."

If you accept Cowboy's offer, turn to PAGE 19.

If you don't accept it, settle down for a nap instead.

The snake is gone!

In its place lies a lovely blue-and-silver snakeskin purse.

Whatever evil rode the rails this day has vanished.

"Want to play Go Fish with me?" asks the little girl, holding up a deck of cards.

"Sure," you say, grinning. "You know, you remind me of my sister, Mary."

"Yeah?"

"Yeah."

You kick the snakeskin purse under the seat and sit down beside her.

You can hardly wait to get to Aunt Kate's.

THE END

"Sorry," you mumble to Beautiful Lady. "The train jerked. I'll close it again."

You reach down to close the door, but she grabs your arm.

"Don't touch it!" she says. Her face is ashen. She nudges something into your ribs. You look down and see a small, pearl-handled revolver.

"Move," she whispers. "Walk with me to the back of the train. One false move, and I'll shoot."

She kicks the carrier door shut with her foot.

"Move!"

If you decide to do as she says, turn to PAGE 102.

If you choose to make a run for it, turn to PAGE 103.

You walk with L. Smythe through two cars to the crowded diner. There is a table for four available. You seat yourself by the window. She carefully positions the pet carrier on the seat across from you and sits in the aisle chair beside it.

You pick up the menu and order pepperoni pizza and root beer. L. Smythe orders a crab cocktail and French fries.

When the waiter leaves, she leans across the table.

"Your encounter with Le Main in the coach did not escape me," she snarls. "Since I now know that you are his accomplice, I must warn you that the carrier has its own protection system. An automatic dart thrower is now aimed at your right eye. I would prefer to take you in alive, but I will not hesitate to trigger the release mechanism if you give me any trouble. One wrong move, and it's curtains! The dart is poison!"

"But . . ." you protest nervously. "I'm not his accomplice. I'm on my way to Twin Falls to visit my Aunt Kate."

"Excuse me," says a voice at your elbow. "Is this seat taken?"

Scarface — or Le Main — is standing beside you.

If you invite Scarface to sit down, turn to PAGE 22.

If you tell him the seat is taken, turn to PAGE 23.

You and Beautiful Lady change seats. You are trying to remember your International Morse Code so you will know what Scarface was telling you.

Pinch — squeeze — squeeze — pinch.

That's P.

Pinch.

E.

Squeeze.

T.

PET!

It must have something to do with her pet carrier.

You look at the metal cage, then over at Beautiful Lady, who is filling a hypodermic needle from a small vial. She has placed the gun on her lap while she prepares the injection. You know she is up to no good.

Should you open the pet carrier or try to get her gun?

If you grab the gun, turn to PAGE 52.

If you opt to open the pet carrier, turn to PAGE 101.

"It is time to go," says Beautiful Lady, getting up. "Bring our young hostage along for security."

She picks up the pet carrier and starts down the aisle.

Scarface forces you from your seat. Something digs into the small of your back. You think it's a gun, but you're not sure.

"March!" he says gruffly.

Are you going to march? Then turn to PAGE 57.

Thinking about resisting? Turn to PAGE 46.

"Hello," you say, smiling at Beautiful Lady. "What kind of a pet do you have in there?"

You lean over to look through the mesh door, and the sunflower seeds fall out of your pocket and catch on the door handle of the carrier.

She doesn't reply, but that doesn't stop you. Lots of adults don't answer civil questions. This is nothing new.

Her cold clear eyes bore into you, as if she were casting some kind of evil spell.

So much for her! If she won't tell you — then you'll just have to sneak a quick look for yourself!

Sneak a quick look at PAGE 14. √

You move forward in the aisle, holding the seat backs as you proceed cautiously to the front of the car. Your hand inadvertently brushes up against a passenger's head as you grasp the seat.

"Excuse me," you say.

The woman does not move or acknowledge your apology.

What is going on? You can barely put one foot in front of the other. Your mind is moving in slow motion.

But a small part of you is resisting the grogginess. You wonder what that "anti-venin" pill Beautiful Lady gave you really was. Was it some kind of drug to get you under her control? You must get away!

You look back at Beautiful Lady. She is holding a strange-looking calculator and staring right back at you. What is she up to now?

You're not going to wait around to find out! You force yourself ahead and see the snake coiling itself around the neck of a little girl sleeping on one of the seats. Do you have time to save her? If only you weren't so groggy!

If you decide to leave the little girl for now, turn to PAGE 8.

If you decide to try to rescue the girl despite your confusion, turn to PAGE 28.

Why should you get involved with this snake business when you're on vacation? You give a quick glance at the floor as you hurry to the end of the car. When you reach the door, you yank it open and keep right on going through to the next car, which is not nearly as crowded as the one you left.

You find an empty double seat and sprawl out across it, facing the window so you can see the scenery.

Maybe you'll have a chance to raft on the Snake River when you get to Aunt Kate's. One thing for sure. That's the only snake you want to have anything to do with — ever.

THE END

"Two against one isn't fair!" you yell, tackling Scarface.

Your action catches him by surprise.

"Make you a deal," he whispers as you wrestle him to the floor. "Let me go, and we'll cut you in on the jewels."

You hold him there, arms pinned back, while you consider the offer.

"They're worth half a million," he adds. "You can be a full partner."

The offer is tempting. You'd like the freedom that goes with one-third of half a million. On the other hand, your mother probably won't like it. There's never been a criminal in the family before.

"The old lady's really a cop from Boston," mutters Scarface.

If you can figure out what one-third of half a million is, you may turn to PAGE 81.

If you can't, turn to PAGE 78.

You know Scarface and Beautiful Lady will kill you eventually, but you don't think they'll choose to do it on a train.

You think of your stubborn dog, Minnie, and how she refuses to go out to the yard when you want her to. So you pull "a Minnie" and drop to the floor, totally limp.

"You dumb kid!" Scarface yells, trying to pull you up. "Get going! Get moving!"

He sounds just like you when you're talking to Minnie.

Beautiful Lady screams at Scarface, "Look out!"

You look up from the floor. Elderly Lady has tackled Scarface and knocked him into one of the seats. Beautiful Lady picks up the pet carrier and starts to run.

"Grab her!" Elderly Lady yells.

You jump up after Beautiful Lady. She must not reach the door. You grab the pet carrier. You know she won't leave without it.

Elderly Lady ties up Scarface and hurries toward you. She handcuffs Beautiful Lady and shakes your hand.

"She" is Eliot Lansing, special agent for the Boston police.

Later that year, you receive a $500 reward for your part in the daring capture. It will help pay your fare to Aunt Kate's next year.

Next summer you'll fly.

THE END

With a smooth movement, you grab the handle and yank open the door of the carrier to see what the cry is about.

Beautiful Lady karate-chops your shoulder, but her action comes too late to stop you. Reeling from the blow, you feel something swoop by you as you strain to focus.

A gorgeous green bird flies past.

There's a racket in the coach. People who sat in stony silence when you got on the train are now ducking, hooting, and laughing as the great green bird swoops up and down the length of the coach, crying: "Help! Help! Help!"

You feel like a fool.

Please turn to PAGE 25.

"Don't let her swallow it!" screams Elderly Lady, who is now a mustached person in pumps. He reaches over the seat to grab the bottle of pills just as the green parrot comes swooping by and knocks him off balance.

You are not sure how to separate the good guys from the bad guys on this train. You think you might put your money on the parrot.

"Stop her!" yells Elderly Lady again.

Do you really want to get involved?

If you decide to stop Beautiful Lady from taking the pill, turn to PAGE 70.

If you decide to forget the whole mishmash and stay under the seat until you get to Idaho, turn to PAGE 71.

You climb over a packing case and stretch out across the top of a steamer trunk to reach the cage. You place your ear on the top of the carrier and listen intently. There is no sound or movement. Perhaps the poor animal is already dead.

You reach down and grab the handle just as a beam of light crosses the interior of the car. You turn to see where it's coming from.

Someone is entering the baggage car!

The light disappears as the heavy door closes again, but you have seen the visitor.

It is Beautiful Lady.

You lie very still and quiet on top of the trunk.

"I know you are there!" she says, her voice echoing in the car. "I warn you. Do not open my pet carrier!"

You peer through the darkness. She is holding a gun, but she does not seem to know exactly where you are. When she speaks, she is facing a side wall.

Her eyes have not yet adjusted to the dark.

If you decide to open the carrier anyway, turn to PAGE 62.

If you decide to stay still, turn to PAGE 5.

On the other hand, you could be in plenty of trouble just being in the baggage car. You certainly are not authorized personnel.

But you're curious about the cage.

You crawl over the baggage to get next to it and stretch out on top of a trunk so you can look inside.

At first, you think the two glowing green spots inside are the eyes of a caged animal, but then you realize they are tiny lights on a small computer.

Could this be the danger that Scarface meant?

Should you open it?

You *are* relieved that it's not a suffering animal, all cooped up.... But you've always been interested in electronics.... Maybe you should open it just to be *certain* that it's not an animal. Maybe you were mistaken.... Why would someone put a computer in a cage?

You unlatch the door and swing it open. There is a diagram on the side wall that says:

BEHAVIOR MODIFICATION UNIT
EXTREME DANGER — DO NOT TOUCH

You've gone this far. If you decide to touch it, turn to PAGE 88.

If you decide to close the door and leave, turn to PAGE 92.

"No!" you yell at Beautiful Lady, reaching across to knock the needle from her hand.

In your haste, your can of cherry soda spills — right into Beautiful Doctor's open handbag.

The needle drops to the floor. Then suddenly her purse sputters and pops and starts smoking. Your soda has drenched her calculator.

Beautiful Lady leaps up and runs down the aisle.

"Stop her!" Scarface yells, lunging from his seat.

You are happy to see that he has made a miraculous recovery.

Beautiful Lady is detained by train personnel, while Scarface comes back to speak to you. The purse is still smoking and hissing, but the lights on the calculator have gone out.

"My cherry soda gummed up the works," you say apologetically. "My mother was right. Too much sugar."

"You saved my life!" says Scarface. "Thank goodness you deactivated it in time!"

Please turn to PAGE 64.

You jump from the seat and grab Beautiful Lady's gun.

"Drop it!" you say to her as she is about to plunge the needle into Scarface's arm.

She looks at you through narrowed eyes, as if to call your bluff. This action makes you furious. Nobody ever thinks that kids are serious.

"I'm serious!" you yell.

She glances away from you to the pet carrier on the floor.

Suddenly, it becomes clear. The key to this mystery is in that cage. You whirl and fire at the pet carrier. There is a shower of sparks and then a puff of smoke. Then, nothing but a sizzling noise.

Scarface leaps to his feet. "Thank you!" he yells. "She is a neurological specialist — my former assistant. She was controlling my mind!"

"I know," you say calmly, gathering up your lunch and your crossword puzzle book. "I figured it out."

"You have a wonderful mind!" says Scarface, staring at you. "Would you like to participate in one of our experiments?"

"Not this summer," you reply. "I'm going to my Aunt Kate's."

You take your belongings and move to another coach.

THE END

The baggage car is hot and dark. You trip over a trunk, regain your balance, and stand still in the humid, musty car to allow your eyes to adjust to the shadows.

Then, you gingerly pick your way through, eyeing the belongings of your fellow passengers. You spot your own old, brown leather bag with its tarnished buckle, wedged in between a sleek, red Naugahyde suitcase and a metal box of some sort.

Scarface's message flashes into your mind.

DANGER IN BOX!

Swell, you tell yourself.

There are a score of boxes of varying shapes and sizes in here.

But there is something special about the one beside your suitcase. You move closer to examine it. It is an exact replica of Beautiful Lady's pet carrier.

You are outraged that anyone would allow a pet to ride in this dark, stifling car. It could die before reaching its destination! Maybe you should open the cage and free the animal.

If you choose to release the animal, turn to PAGE 49.

If you decide it's none of your business, turn to PAGE 50.

54

You lean back in your seat, keeping an eye on Scarface, who is seated across the aisle. You figure that it is only a matter of time until he starts talking again.

You are right.

"You've had it, kid," says the voice coming from the carrier. "You are doomed!"

This time, you don't look at the cage but at Scarface's throat. It moves, just like Buddy Hensley's did on amateur night at school.

You start to leave, but Beautiful Lady restrains you by putting a hand on your knee.

"Would you like to see the sports section?" she asks, handing you another part of the paper.

"No — I'm getting off here," you reply.

The train is grinding to a jerky stop, and passengers are moving down the aisle.

"I don't think you are," she says ominously, looking across the aisle at Scarface.

Turn to PAGE 27, please.

You remove Scarface's hand and move across the aisle. Beautiful Lady sits down by Scarface. She takes his pulse, then leans across the aisle to reach into her purse, which is in the seat beside you. She pulls out a stethoscope.

Quite inadvertently, you glance down and notice that in addition to a stethoscope, her handbag also contains a gun and a small calculator.

Strange equipment for a medical doctor, you think.

Well, you can justify the calculator. She needs that to keep track of her income. But what about the gun? You're sure that there's a law against shooting patients who are too sick to be treated.

Slyly, you steal another peek in the handbag. The calculator looks different than those you've seen before. This one is flashing green and amber lights. You'd like a closer look. Something strange is going on here.

If you decide to take the calculator from her purse, turn to PAGE 73.

If you suppress your curiosity and leave it there, turn to PAGE 97.

"Oh, I'm quite comfortable here," you say to Beautiful Lady.

Scarface squeezes your arm again. You're not sure, but you think he's saying *thanks.* You open your crossword puzzle book and pretend to be busy with a puzzle.

"I insist that you move," says Beautiful Lady coldly.

If there's anything you hate, it's bossy people. You look across at her, ready with a heated reply, when you realize that she is holding a small revolver. So much for your heated reply.

Scarface is squeezing your arm again, and this time, it hurts. He is going to have to let go of your arm if you are to do what Beautiful Lady says. Surely, he must realize that!

But he's not letting go!

Pinch . . . squeeze . . . squeeze . . . pinch.

Is he trying to tell you something?

Pinch.

"Ouch!"

Squeeze.

"Okay!"

Yes! He's spelling out a word.

"Move!" commands Beautiful Lady.

"I'm moving, I'm moving," you say as Scarface releases your arm.

So what's holding you back? Move to
PAGE 39.

You move down the aisle ahead of Scarface. You plan to make a run for it as soon as you get to the crowded platform, but you don't get that far.

Elderly Lady, who is really a Boston police office in disguise, tackles Scarface from behind. In the resulting scuffle, Scarface's gun goes off and shoots you in the foot.

Beautiful Lady and the pet carrier vanish into the crowd on the station platform.

Scarface gets ten years in the slammer. Beautiful Lady and the jewels are never found. Your foot heals slowly.

Your summer in Idaho has been ruined.

From now on, you'll pay more attention to your horoscope when it says, "Postpone all trips until tomorrow."

THE END

"That's okay," you say, trying to act non-chalant. You close your eyes and lean back.

"Suit yourself," he drawls. He picks up his guitar and starts to sing:

> There was a sharp gal on a train
> Who made it perfectly plain
> Her pet not to touch
> But you don't listen much
> Oh, you'll never pull that trick
>   again, again
> You'll never pull that trick again.
>
> There was a young lady in red
> With silver blonde curls on her
>   head.
> She looked luscious to some
> But was packin' a gun
> Li'l pardner, yer jist about dead,
>   yes, sirree
> Li'l pardner, yer jist about dead.
>
> Her pet ain't a cat or a dog
> Or a moose or a rat or a frog.
> Her cage carries cash
> From the Bank in Salash
> Now this ditty is yer epilogue,
> Oh, this ditty is yer epilogue.

As the words sink in, you sit up with a jerk, but it's too late. She's coming toward you, toting the pet carrier.

If you decide to run, turn to PAGE 84.

If you decide to scream for the conductor, turn to PAGE 89.

As you reach for the sunflower seeds, the train lurches, and your hand hits the door handle of the pet carrier. The package of seeds falls to the floor, and the door slowly swings open.

Now is your chance to see Beautiful Lady's pet!

As you lean down, you hear her gasp.

If you decide to let your curiosity rule, turn to PAGE 14.

If you decide not to peek, turn to PAGE 36.

You get down on your hands and knees and crawl under the seat in front of you, searching for your apple. While you are down there, you notice something very strange. Elderly Lady, in the purple hat, has very muscular, hairy legs — and a stiletto is tucked in the side of her black, knee-length nylons!

Please turn to PAGE 13.

Things are quite different in the coach than when you left. Beautiful Lady is handcuffed to the seat, and Scarface is barking orders at several of the passengers, who are obeying automatically. Beautiful Lady's pet carrier is open, and inside you can see another computer — a duplicate of the one you just shut off in the baggage car. Scarface approaches you.

"Miller here, secret agent," he says, shaking your hand. "These are my people." He looks over at Beautiful Lady. "Except her. She's an enemy spy with a doctoral degree in behavior control. She thought she had us this time, but thanks to you — we'll get to our project site with our full faculties!"

"That computer's a decoy. No wiring in it. But I caught on to that too late. Thanks for your help."

"Don't mention it," you say.

"Where is your project site?" you ask.

"Twin Falls, Idaho," he replies, without looking up

Twin Falls! Right in Aunt Kate's backyard. You groan quietly as you pick up your crossword puzzle book and try to concentrate.

"This is my lucky day," you mumble sarcastically.

"That so?" he replies.

He doesn't smile.

THE END

"You are mean and cruel!" you yell to Beautiful Lady. You drop down behind the pet carrier for protection. "I'll report you to the ASPCA!"

Your voice gives away your position, and two shots ring out just as you swing open the door of the cage.

You feel the sting of one bullet as it enters your arm . . . the other zings into the cage.

There is a bright flash of light, and, inside the pet carrier, you see a small computer, damaged beyond repair by the blast.

There was no animal!

Beautiful Lady gasps and turns to run, but is unable to open the heavy metal door. Despite your wound, you scramble over the baggage and tackle her.

Just as you subdue her, the door squeaks open, and you see Scarface framed in the opening. Behind him is the conductor.

What now?

You may be in trouble.

If you think you are, turn to PAGE 104.

If you think you are and don't care, turn to PAGE 104.

(PAGE 104 can handle any situation.)

"What is it?" you ask Scarface.

"A remote unit to control a computer in the baggage car."

"The box?" you ask, thinking of the message he wrote.

He nods. "I didn't think we had a chance of getting the unit from her purse. I can't thank you enough! She had me almost totally under her control!"

"No thanks needed," you say. "Glad to help. By the way, who are you?"

"Doctor Solem Fishbine, head of experimental neurological services at St. Michael's. She used to be my assistant, but we had to let her go when she started experimenting on bank personnel. She almost cleaned out the Pennsylvania Main Trust that way — controlling tellers' minds so they would add four zeros to her checks."

"What's in the pet carrier?" you ask.

"A gray poodle named Brain." He smiles at you. "Say, how'd you like to sit with me the rest of the way?"

"Thanks, but I think I'll go up to the next coach and look for a friend who got on at the last stop."

He knows you're lying, but you don't care.

You'd really like to be in control of your own mind when you get to Idaho.

THE END

Obviously, Elderly Lady is not elderly — and not a lady, either, with those hairy legs and that stiletto. He must be the accomplice.

The train has pulled into a station and most of the passengers in your coach are filing out. You start to get up, but Beautiful Lady puts her hand on your knee.

"Did you find the newspaper interesting?" she asks.

You can feel your ears getting red, as they always do when you tell a lie.

"Not very," you mumble.

"Not even page three?"

"I don't remember."

Everyone else has left the coach. There are just the two of you plus Elderly Lady and Scarface, who is still sitting down.

You suspect that Beautiful Lady knows that you know.

If you decide to make a run for it, turn to PAGE 31.

If you decide to stay and keep an eye on the thieves until you can get help, turn to PAGE 33. ✓

Gagging because you don't like to take pills at all — especially not without something to drink — you choke down the pill.

Your head stops aching immediately, and you turn to Beautiful Lady to thank her.

She smiles brightly at you and pats your hand.

Maybe you had her figured out wrong after all. She no longer appears to be evil.

"I'd better get your pet back," you say, feeling very remorseful but not very brave. "It's the least I can do."

She smiles at you. "No problem," she says.

You smile back, but wonder how in the world you are going to even find the snake. You stall just a little to muster some courage, then stand up and point to the front of the car. "It went this way," you announce with certainty.

Beautiful Lady shakes her head. "You are mistaken," she contradicts. "It went to the rear."

Your head has stopped hurting, but you feel confused. You are sure the snake moved to the front.

If you decide to follow your own recollection, turn to PAGE 42.

If you decide to go to the rear on the advice of Beautiful Lady, turn to PAGE 72.

Later that summer, a telegram arrives for you in care of your Aunt Kate. You excitedly tear open the yellow envelope.

> The Secret Service invites you to be its honored guest at a reception in Washington, D.C., on September 7th at 7:00 P.M.

You, your Aunt Kate, and your mother fly to Washington to attend. You are awarded the Medal of Meritorious Assistance and made an honorary member of the Secret Service. A state dinner is held in your honor.

The menu is pepperoni pizza and root beer.

THE END

You spit out the pill and lurch from your seat, stumbling into the aisle. Not even Scarface or Elderly Lady is watching you now. You look around warily.

Where did the snake go?

You stare at the rubber runner in the aisle, and it slowly undulates up and down as if it were moving on a track.

Perhaps the snake is underneath? . . .

You've got to get out of here!

The rubber runner moves again.

Is it your eyes or the snake?

You'd like to sit down and tuck your feet up under your chin — but you'd like to get the conductor, too!

You hear a hiss behind you. Beautiful Lady has uncapped a vial, and a slow spiral of blue gas is wafting through the coach!

Elderly Lady wags a finger at you.

"Sit by me, dearie," she says in a monotone.

If you yelled at your little brother this morning, you go to bed without dinner. Turn to PAGE 21.

If you don't have a little brother to yell at, you don't know what you're missing. Turn to PAGE 20.

You run toward the doorway, chasing the bird. But your efforts are futile. While the passengers are waiting for the conductor to lead them out, the green bird soars out over their heads — dipping, diving, enjoying its freedom.

It flies to the top of a water tank beside the station house, looks back at you, and glides off into the sky. You wave once and watch until it becomes a tiny speck, then disappears.

When you go back into the coach, Elderly Lady identifies himself. He is with Interpol, and Beautiful Lady is a foreign agent. The green bird, he explains, has a canister of microfilm that contains important infor-mation attached under its wing.

"I'm sorry," you say as you look at his dejected face. "The bird got away."

But you're not sorry at all.

You never did like caged birds.

THE END

You glance at the apple in your hand, then let fly a slow change-up that hits the target and knocks the pill bottle to the floor.

Elderly Lady kicks free of the pumps and vaults over the seat. He handcuffs Beautiful Lady to his own wrist and leans forward to speak.

"Get the parrot," he orders, "while I keep an eye on Red Bird here."

You hesitate. The whistle blows, and you feel the train slow down.

"We're coming to a station. Hurry! That bird must not get away!"

The train is slowing down, and people are heading for the doorway. Once the door is open, you know the bird will be the first to exit.

If you decide to capture the bird, turn to PAGE 98.

If you decide to let it fly free, turn to PAGE 69.

You watch cautiously from under the seat. Elderly lady swings his knitting bag at Beautiful Lady and knocks the bottle of pills to the floor.

"Rats," says Beautiful Lady in a nasty voice. "Now I've had it."

Elderly lady crawls over the seat, handcuffs Beautiful Lady, then collects the pills from the floor.

"Memory Erasers," he explains. (By now, it's obvious to you that Elderly Lady is really a middle-aged man.) "She is a spy from the State of Eruka. The Bureau will want to question her!"

You look up from under the seat and nod.

For a fleeting moment you wish you had one of the memory eraser pills. This whole trip has been like a bad movie you want to forget.

He grabs the bird as it swoops by and deftly unhinges a small film capsule that is banded to one of its legs. He puts the bird back in the carrier and snaps the door shut.

From inside the cage, you hear a muffled cry.

"Help, help!"

This time you know better. You're not going to risk your life for some talking bird. You crawl out from under the seat and head for the lounge car.

THE END

You shrug your shoulders and move to the rear as Beautiful Lady suggests, but you don't see any sign of the blue-and-silver snake.

You realize you will have to get down on the floor and look under the seats for the snake. But maybe you should drop the whole thing and get out of this crazy situation. Suppose you just keep going right on through to the coach behind?

You glance back at Beautiful Lady.

She is staring at you.

If you decide to get down on the floor to look, turn to PAGE 107.

If you decide to hurry through to the next coach, turn to PAGE 44.

While Beautiful Lady is putting the stethoscope around her neck, you slip your hand in her purse, and carefully avoiding the gun, you remove the calculator. As you do so, your fingers hit the *off* button. The flashing lights cease, but even more startling, Scarface lunges out of his seat, and Beautiful Lady runs down the aisle.

"Stop her!" Scarface yells at the conductor, who is just entering the coach.

Beautiful Lady is detained by train personnel, while Scarface comes back to where you are sitting.

"You saved my life," he says, patting your shoulder.

He points to the calculator. "Would you please hand me that ... very, very carefully?" he asks.

Now, very, very carefully, turn to PAGE 64.

Your brain whirls into motion. You don't think Beautiful Lady saw Le Main pass you the note, but you can't take a chance on ignoring his warning. However, you think his suggestion to run will only call unwanted attention to yourself.

You decide to play it cool.

You must pass through one more coach before you reach the dining car. You know what you are going to do.

You are going to turn to PAGE 106.

"I am hungry," you admit to L. Smythe.

She smiles. "Good. I hate to eat alone."

She rummages through her large handbag again and pulls out a silver pouch, from which she extracts a folded sheet. She shakes the sheet open and covers the pet carrier. It reminds you of your grandmother covering her canary's cage at night.

"There," she whispers. "That will prevent contamination."

She stands and picks up the pet carrier, waiting for you to step into the aisle.

"Are you taking that with you?" you inquire, frowning.

"I cannot leave it unattended," she whispers. She nods toward Scarface. "That man is a foreign agent."

You do not want to get too close to the pet carrier, so you stand aside to let her lead the way. As you do, Scarface slips a note into your hand. As L. Smythe and the pet carrier proceed down the aisle, you steal a quick look at the note.

RUN! YOU ARE IN DANGER! SHE IS A FOREIGN SPY!

LE MAIN, SECRET SERVICE

Whom should you believe?

If you decide to proceed to the dining car with L. Smythe, turn to PAGE 38.

If you decide to escape on your way to the dining car, look over to PAGE 74.

"No thanks," you say to Beautiful Lady, thinking that you will move to another coach and get away from this strange woman.

You don't believe her story. Anyone can buy a fake ID card at a variety store. Why, you have one in your wallet right now that says you're a member of the FBI! As a matter of fact, you saw something on TV last night about a woman spy who had used false credentials to infiltrate Fort Benjamin Harrison in Indiana. She escaped with a vital component for a secret weapon. She even looked like Beautiful Lady — except the lady on TV had black hair.

Maybe . . .

You stare at her blonde curls and detect what seems to be a piece of fabric just behind her ear.

Of course! She is wearing a wig!

It is as if Beautiful Lady is reading your mind.

"I can tell that you know who I am," she says slowly. "Come with me. You are much too smart for your own good."

You feel something poke into your side and look down to see a small pearl-handled revolver.

If you had pizza for breakfast, turn to PAGE 102.

If you didn't have pizza for breakfast, turn to PAGE 102.

Go to PAGE 102!

"Forget it," you say to the conductor. "Just kidding."

"I should put you off at the next stop for telling a whopper like that," the conductor mutters. He moves down the aisle, grumbling about kids. When he gets out of earshot, Cowboy speaks to you from under his Stetson.

"The one with the gun — is she wearin' a red dress and carryin' a pet cage with her?" he asks.

Please go to PAGE 32.

"I need some handcuffs for this one!" you yell at the cop from Boston as he handcuffs Beautiful Lady to the coach door.

Together, you handcuff Scarface and prop him up in one of the seats.

"I never could have done it without you," the officer says, shaking your hand. "Could you do me one more favor?"

"Sure," you reply. "Name it."

"I'd like to get out of these clothes," he says, looking with embarrassment at his polyester print dress and mid-heeled pumps. "Will you keep an eye on these two while I change?"

"I'd be glad to," you say.

He picks up his knitting bag and goes off to the washroom.

Later that summer, you get a check for $500 from the gem merchant in Boston, and you and your Aunt Kate eat steak for the rest of the month.

THE END

"Come with me, and I will!" you declare to the conductor.

"Waste of time," he mutters, skeptically. "I just came through there, and I didn't see any lady with a gun."

"She was wearing a red dress," you explain. "And she has a pet carrier with her."

If you have a red dress, turn to PAGE 34.
If you wouldn't be caught dead in a red dress, turn to PAGE 34 anyway.

"Deal!" you say to Scarface.

You both shake hands, then you let Scarface get up.

He ties up the cop from Boston, puts a gag on him, and props him up on one of the seats. Beautiful Lady grabs the pet carrier, and you hurry off the train just as it pulls away from the station.

You feel heady with excitement now that you have embarked on a life of crime.

"Where to now?" you ask.

"Never-never land," says Beautiful Lady, pulling a gun. "I don't plan to split this loot with anyone!"

She fires quickly—once at you and once at Scarface. You sink to the platform, unable to stop her as she hails a cab, drives off with the jewels, and is never seen again.

"Is there no honor among thieves?" Scarface asks plaintively.

"No," you say sadly. "Crime does not pay," you add wisely.

Scarface gets thirty years for armed robbery. You get fifteen for aiding criminals.

As you recover from your gunshot wounds in the hospital, you disguise yourself as a nurse and, while your guard is asleep, walk right out the front door. Instead of serving fifteen years in prison, you devote the rest of your life to medicine.

THE END

"Thanks," you say to Cowboy, "but I can handle this without a gun."

You enter the coach and stride down the aisle, Cowboy on your heels.

"Excuse me, ma'am," you say politely when you reach Beautiful Lady's seat. "I'd like my lunch bag, please."

She turns and smiles at you.

"Surely," she replies, handing you the bag. "You left in such a hurry! I don't bite, you know."

You frown, uncertain as to whether or not her friendliness is sincere.

The revolver is nowhere in sight.

Let your eyes drift over to PAGE 83.

"I thought you wanted to see my pet," she continues.

"Well ... I ... I ..." you stammer.

This is a switch! Is it a trick?

"Well, do you or don't you?"

She smiles warmly and pats your hand.

"Well, yes!" you say, trying to control your excitement. "I love animals."

"Good," she replies. "You'll adore Ralph."

She reaches down and unhinges the door. "You'll have to get down and peek in," she says. "Ralph's shy. He only comes out at night."

To make Ralph's acquaintance, turn to PAGE 93.

You dart out of the seat and run, expecting at any moment to feel the bullet in your back.

"Stop! Thief!"

Beautiful Lady, who is in red, is pointing a finger at you and screaming at the conductor.

(Rats! She is stealing your other option.)

The conductor and two burly sailors stop your flight.

"He has my money!" Beautiful Lady tearfully cries.

"I do not!" you say indignantly. "Search me!"

They do, and in your back pocket they find a roll of one-hundred-dollar bills, which Beautiful Lady must have planted on you. Or perhaps it was Cowboy?

No matter. You've run out of choices. You've been set up!

Cowboy and Beautiful Lady ride off to Idaho with their pet carrier full of stolen bills.

And you?

They turn you over to the sheriff at the next stop, and you're hauled off to a Colorado jail. You get six years.

A summer with Aunt Kate will have to wait.

THE END

You go for broke. What have you got to lose? You know Beautiful Lady will do you in, either here or between cars.

You're not going through that door!

You pretend to reach for the metal handle, but instead give Beautiful Lady a sharp elbow in her beautiful ribs.

You don't even hear the shot. The gun must have a silencer. You put your hand to your rib cage and feel warm, wet blood oozing from the wound.

But this is your lucky day.

Scarface comes to your rescue. The railroad police quickly overpower Beautiful Lady and take her into custody. Elderly Lady hurries to your side. She is none other than Dr. Amelia Cartiledgiani, famous Italian surgeon, on her way to Twin Falls, Idaho, to deliver a paper to the American College of Surgeons, Northwest Branch.

Using a trunk in the baggage car as an operating table, she performs emergency surgery and saves your life.

You arrive at Aunt Kate's very hungry.

THE END

"Let's go," you say to Cowboy after a few minutes.

He hands you a deputy's badge, which you tuck in your pocket. Then you accompany Marshal Westrock back through the train to the bank robbers' car. You strap on the spare six-shooter, which was stashed in his guitar, and rehearse your plan for capture.

Marshal Westrock will take Beautiful Lady and Studs Monigan.

You get Scarface and the conductor.

You enter the car. The conductor is talking to Scarface.

"Freeze!" you shout, pointing your gun at them.

Scarface offers no resistance. The conductor tries to run, but you stick out your foot. He trips and falls in the aisle, blocking Studs Monigan's escape. You hold the gun on Scarface until Marshal Westrock throws you a coil of rope. You tie them securely and turn to help the Marshal, but he has already subdued his pair and handcuffed them to the train seat.

You spend the rest of your journey drinking root beer and playing poker with Marshal Westrock.

Aunt Kate is very impressed with your deputy's badge.

THE END

"No thanks," you tell Cowboy. "I'd rather stay here and drink root beer."

"Suit yourself," he says, getting up. "Nice meetin' you."

He tips his ten-gallon hat and leaves the car, and you turn to look out the window. As you watch the scenery, you see a flash of red in the glass.

You whirl around in your seat.

Too late.

Beautiful Lady pulls the trigger. She is a good shot.

You slump to the floor, your root beer in your hand.

There goes your summer vacation.

THE END

88

You look more closely at the diagram. It seems to have two systems, and the wiring is designed in a strange egg shape. Among the many labels, you see R LOBE, L LOBE, CRANIAL CONTROL.

Suddenly it becomes clear!

If this is Beautiful Lady's pet carrier, she is using it to control someone's brain. Maybe her target is Scarface!

You reach in and switch the unit off, and without even closing the door, you dash from the baggage car back to your coach.

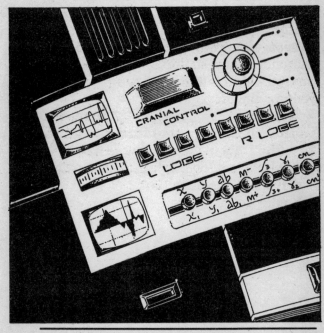

Will Scarface smile now? Turn to PAGE 61.

You jump up from your seat.

"Conductor!" you yell. "It's her! The woman with the gun!"

People turn to look—first at you, then at Beautiful Lady coming toward you. Cowboy puts down his guitar.

"Arrest her!" you holler. You back out of the seat, thinking of the song lyrics. "Arrest them both! They've robbed the Salash Bank. The cash is in her pet carrier!"

She is almost beside you now. The conductor is moving cautiously toward you, gesturing to Cowboy for help.

Together, the men seize your arms and subdue you. They send a porter to wire ahead to the next station, and you are bodily transported from the train and placed in a waiting ambulance.

"I'm not crazy!" you yell. But as the ambulance pulls away, you look up and see Beautiful Lady in the window seat by Cowboy. She is petting a silver-gray poodle.

Perhaps its name is Cash.

You're not crazy.

Are you?

THE END

You know this is your last chance.

You give Beautiful Lady a mighty shove, setting her off balance, and scramble over the Dutch door. For a second, you hang outside the train by your fingertips, watching the rocky ground rush by your feet as the speeding train passes through a mountain tunnel.

Sunlight again. This is it!

You let go and drop to the ground, rolling over and over, away from the tracks. You lie there, exhausted from the exertion, and watch the train disappear. As it does, you see Beautiful Lady waving her gun and yelling at you from the door of the speeding train.

Now you know.

It was all a bluff. Her gun wasn't loaded, or she would have shot you.

Slowly, you sit up to investigate your condition. You are sore all over. Your right arm is broken, but better your arm than your leg. It's a long walk to Idaho.

THE END

You're not about to seek out trouble on this trip. You're looking forward to a summer in Idaho with no parental strings. You swing the door shut and start climbing over the baggage to the exit door. As you go, you try to figure out what is going on.

You crawl over a trunk. You push your way around a stack of boxes, but you're getting tired. It must be the heat. You're moving with very jerky motions — mechanically.

Suddenly it hits you! Beautiful Lady is somehow controlling Scarface, and maybe even you! That must be why you're suddenly so groggy.

You open your mouth to shout, but no noise comes through. Beautiful Lady's behavior modification unit is controlling you, too. You must get back to that computer! Turn it off!

You crawl back and strain to reach the door. You can barely grasp the handle. One finger catches it. The door swings open. You fight against losing control as you make a supreme effort to hit the activator switch.

OFF!

You made it.

Welcome back from robot-land.

THE END

You squat down and peer into the cage as Beautiful Lady suggests. The interior is black. You lean forward, squinting to adjust your eyes to the dark. There's something furry inside, and it's flapping frantically.

Zap! Two needlelike stings hit your throat.

Your neck! Something has you by the neck!

It's a bat. As you start to lose consciousness forever, you realize that Ralph is no ordinary pet. It isn't even an ordinary bat. Beautiful Lady's prized pet is a vampire!

As you fade out under the seat and out of sight of the other passengers, you hear her tinkling laughter through the rumble of the train.

"Sit down with me, pet," you hear her say to Cowboy. "I don't bite."

You try to yell to warn him, but no sound will come.

Beautiful Lady doesn't bite. But her pet does!

You know it's only a matter of time until Cowboy joins you. And he won't need a coach seat where he's going!

THE END

"You bet I want to take a look," you say bravely to Cowboy. "She's dangerous! She should be hauled off and locked up."

You stride down the aisle with Cowboy loping along behind.

Cowboy taps your shoulder just before you enter Beautiful Lady's coach.

"Wait, pardner! Better do some thinkin' here. How're ya plannin' to corral this gun-totin' lady? You'd better strap on one of my six-shooters."

He unbuckles his gun belt and offers it to you.

You hesitate. You don't much like the idea of shooting anybody—but it's not too smart to be unarmed, either.

If you decide to go with your wits instead of his gun, turn to PAGE 82.

If you decide you'd prefer a nap to a shoot-out, close this book, shut your eyes, and wait until you hear the conductor announce "Twin Falls!"

"Then she was going to have them switch our coach to another track where it would be hauled away by a waiting enemy locomotive and put on a ship for Outer Rroberia."

"Kidnapping?" you ask, holding your wounded arm.

Scarface nods. "Mass kidnapping. Every agent in the coach."

"And I almost pulled it off," snarls Beautiful Lady, making an ugly face.

"Almost," says Scarface, handcuffing her. "Except for our clever young friend here!"

He entrusts Beautiful Lady to the custody of the conductor and leads you off to have your wound dressed by an agent-medic.

"You'll get a department citation for this!" he says enthusiastically.

You smile at him.

"There's a moral to all this," you say.

"What's that?" he asks.

"Be kind to animals," you reply.

THE END

You wrench open the door between the coaches and rush to join the passengers who are disembarking. There is a policeman on the platform.

"Officer!" you shout. "The jewel thieves are on the train. They're in that coach!"

You point at the car you just left, and he leaps aboard, gun drawn. You follow, but your help is not needed.

The policeman and Elderly Lady are marching Scarface and Beautiful Lady off the train. Elderly Lady has the pet carrier. Her hat is askew, and under her veil you can see that she has a mustache. She winks as she passes you.

"Undercover agent," she whispers in a man's voice.

But did she really say it?

Scarface is looking at you, too. And his throat is moving again, just like Buddy Hensley's.

You climb back on the train and return to your seat. Your package of sunflower seeds is on the floor. You pick it up and lean back.

One nice thing about having the jewel thieves captured—now you can have a window seat.

THE END

Maybe the calculator is really a beeper, you think. A call system, so the hospital can contact the doctor wherever she is.

But it's not making any noise.

Oh, well, it's none of your business. You reach into your lunch bag and take out a can of cherry soda.

You look across the aisle and see that Beautiful Lady is preparing to give Scarface an injection. Scarface is sitting up so straight that he looks paralyzed.

But he's not.

Your keen eyes detect one muscle in his cheek that is twitching—just the way yours does when you're angry or frightened.

"What are you doing?" you ask Beautiful Lady.

"I'm giving him something to make him better," she says in a patronizing tone.

You frown. You think of the time you went on a camping trip and cut your foot. The hospital wouldn't even give you a tetanus shot without a signed release.

"Doesn't he have to sign something first?" you ask.

"Oh, no," she replies airily.

The muscle in Scarface's cheek is moving rapidly now. Could he be signaling you?

Beautiful Lady raises the needle and you make a snap decision.

Snap over to PAGE 51.

You grab your sunflower seeds and scramble out from under the seat.

"Here, Polly, Polly," you say, scattering a trail of seeds.

The bird pecks cautiously at one, then follows the trail until it is sitting on your arm nibbling at the seeds in your hand.

Elderly Lady offers you his free hand.

"Gustav Anton," he says. "Interpol. You have done the international police a great service, my friend. We have been tracking Red Bird here for three years."

Beautiful Lady scowls at you, but you pretend not to notice.

"She has information that is crucial to world peace."

He pauses and beckons you to bring the bird closer. "And so does her friend."

Go on to PAGE 99.

Gustav Anton, the disguised police agent, reaches up under Polly's wing and detaches a tiny canister.

"Microfiche," he says. "A record of all enemy agents in the Western Hemisphere. Invaluable!"

You put Polly back in the pet carrier and give her some extra sunflower seeds.

Later that year, you are guest of honor at a banquet in Paris sponsored by Interpol. A medal is hung around your neck, and as a special gift you are awarded custody of Polly.

It is good to renew acquaintance with Elderly Lady again, but you hardly recognize him. Gustav has exchanged his purple hat and sling pumps for a British tweed suit.

"Tally-ho!" you say.

"Help!" says Polly.

Obviously, she has not been thoroughly debriefed.

THE END

Beautiful Lady scowls at you.

"I should have known that you were an army brat!" she says.

You smile. "I'm an army brat just like you're a secret service agent," you say. "My father's a plumber in Winfield, Kansas."

She sputters angrily as Scarface leads her away.

When you get to Idaho, you tell Aunt Kate about the incident and the citation you're going to receive. Then one morning, an official-looking packet arrives for you. Excitedly, you tear it open.

Inside is the poison dart and a bill for $86.34 from the railroad, for damage done to the dining coach roof.

You call your lawyer.

It only costs you $600 to win the suit.

THE END

While Beautiful Lady is preoccupied with Scarface, you twist the metal handle on the cage and swing open the door.

Inside is a small computer. You lean forward to read the label pasted on its side:

MIND-CONTROL TERMINAL

PROPERTY OF THE NEUROLOGICAL

RESEARCH BANK, MIAMI, FLORIDA

Of course! You should have guessed! No wonder Scarface was acting like a robot. She was controlling his mind!

You reach in and quickly snap the off button, just as Beautiful Lady moves to inject Scarface.

The results are immediate.

Scarface knocks the syringe from her hand and grabs her gun.

"Thanks!" he says to you. "I'm in the secret service, and she is a foreign agent. You've done your country a great favor today. Thank you! Thank you!"

"You're welcome," you reply.

"Curses," says Beautiful Lady.

You pick up your lunch bag and your crossword puzzle book, and without looking back you go to find another seat in another coach.

Next time you go to Idaho, you'll take a plane.

THE END

Beautiful Lady puts her arm around your waist, and the two of you walk slowly down the narrow aisle. You feel the gun pressing into your ribs.

"I am an excellent shot," she whispers in your ear, smiling for the benefit of the other passengers.

You wonder if the gun is loaded.

You are approaching the Dutch door at the end of the coach.

It may be your last chance to escape this evil lady. On the other hand, she could shoot you right here in the aisle. But would she?

If you refuse to go to the back of the train, turn to PAGE 85.

If you decide to go toward the door, turn to PAGE 90.

You quickly decide that you're not going anywhere with this lady.

"Excuse me," you say in your most polite voice. "But the door to your carrier has jostled open again."

Her head jerks to follow your gaze.

Your diversion works!

As she looks away, you knock the gun to the floor and bolt for the door at the back.

Safe in the next coach, you collapse into a seat beside a cowboy, who is holding a guitar.

"The conductor," you say, panting for breath. "I must find the conductor!"

Cowboy tilts his ten-gallon hat back on his head and smiles at you.

"Yer jist huffin' and puffin' thar, pardner." He strums a chord on his guitar. "Conductor's bunk is up ahead. Go thataway."

"I can't go up there!" you say. "I just came from there. There's a lady with a gun in the car ahead."

Cowboy laughs. "You've been watchin' too much TV, pardner," he says. "Why don't you jist wait here? The conductor will be comin' through." He tips his hat over his face and starts to snore.

You decide that's good advice, but you're annoyed that Cowboy doesn't believe you.

Turn to PAGE 18, please.

104

"Good work!" Scarface says to you in a perfectly normal voice. "I knew I could count on you!"

He puts an arm around your shoulders and smiles. "We'll get that arm looked after right away," he continues.

"I don't get it," you say. "What's going on?"

Scarface sits on a trunk and examines your arm. "You made the mistake of getting into a coach full of secret service people," he explains. "The lady in red here is a double agent, working for another country. Her 'pets' are mind-control computers. The one in the baggage car controlled all the agents in our coach. The one by her side controlled the train crew."

"I get it," you say, hoping that he will continue to explain so you really will understand.

"Once she had reduced us to a robot state," Scarface continues, "she planned to do the same with the train crew. Then . . ."

If you've ever been a double agent, turn to PAGE 95.

If your mother won't let you be a double agent because she says it will stunt your growth, turn to PAGE 95 anyway.

"Excuse me," you say sarcastically to Scarface. "I'm using the pencil."

He stares at you expressionless, neither angry at you nor regretful for his action, and you are aware that there is something unnatural about this man. All his movements are mechanical, much the way a robot's would be.

You move over in your seat—away from him—while you eye the empty seat next to Beautiful Lady. You wonder again about the inhabitant of the pet carrier.

He sees you looking in her direction and shakes his head at you, as if warning you not to move. Slowly, he raises his hand and gestures toward the carrier.

Well. You've had enough of this! You do not look at him, but stuff the package of sunflower seeds in your pocket and move across the aisle.

Please move back through the book to PAGE 41.

You stop near an elderly man wearing thick spectacles. He is seated alone, and on his lap is a duffel bag with T. CARDEN on it.

"Well, Mr. Carden!" you shout. "Imagine meeting you on a train to Twin Falls, Idaho! I haven't seen you for months!"

He squints up at you, struggling to remember who you are. "Yes, yes," he says, "it's . . . it's good to see you again. Here, sit down."

Beautiful Lady turns around to see what is delaying you.

"Thanks for your kind offer," you say to her, "but I'm going to stay here and visit with my old friend!"

Your ruse works.

"As you like," she says frostily. Not wishing to make a scene, she continues down the aisle.

Now you'll never know whether she's a foreign spy or not, but it doesn't matter. If she is, you're safe. If she's not, you have a new adventure ahead.

Well, not exactly an adventure. Mr. Carden can't wait to tell you all about his back trouble and his last two operations. And it's five more hours until you get to Twin Falls. Maybe you should have taken your chances with Beautiful Lady after all!

THE END

Beautiful Lady is watching you expectantly, just as your mother does when she asks if you made your bed.

Reluctantly, you drop to your knees and look under the seats.

You do not look for long.

Her pet is waiting. He zaps you one more time between the eyes and slithers back to his mistress.

Too bad.

As you fade out on the floor, you hazily wonder if you made your bed before you left home this morning.

You'll never know.

THE END